Allyson J. Cat

written by Dandi Daley Knorr
illustrated by Kathryn Hutton

To my Katy

Library of Congress Catalog Card Number 88-63554
Copyright ©1989, by Dandi Daley Knorr
Published by The STANDARD PUBLISHING Company, Cincinnati, Ohio
Division of STANDEX INTERNATIONAL Corporation. Printed in U.S.A.

"But, Mommy, why do *I* have to throw the old pumpkin in the trash?" Katy asked, looking up at her mother.

"Because you shared in the fun of decorating for Halloween," said Mom. "And now you can share in the responsibility of cleaning up. So off you go."

Katy knew it was no use to argue. Mom talked a lot about responsibility.

"We're a family, and we all have our jobs to do at home," Mom always said. "God wants us to be responsible people."

So Katy picked up the soft, carved pumpkin and carried it out the back door.

Ol' jack-o'-lantern doesn't look very scary now, thought Katy.

She crossed her yard to the back where three trash cans stood together like tin men. Katy lifted the lid on the nearest can and dropped in her Halloween pumpkin.

"Look out, Oscar the Grouch," she yelled. "Here it comes!"

As Katy turned to go back to her house, she thought she heard someone crying. She turned back toward the trash can and stood very still.

Katy was about to give up and go home when she heard a muffled "eeyew, eeyew" coming from one of the trash cans.

"Who's in there?" shouted Katy.

Katy lifted the lid from the first can again. There was jack-o'-lantern, but she didn't see anyone crying.

She tried the next can. *Nothing in this can either,* she thought. *Only one trash can left.*

"OK," she said bravely. "I know you're in there!"

Katy lifted the lid off the last trash can and slowly peeked in.

There on top of the garbage was a little gray kitten.

"Eeeyew, eeeyew," it cried.

Katy reached in and pulled out the kitten.

"Oh, you poor thing!" she said. "What are you doing in that trash can? Where's your mommy? I'll bet you're hungry. You come with me."

Katy carried her
discovery into the kitchen.
"Mommy! Come here!
Hurry!" she yelled.

Mother heard the loud
"eeeyew, eeeyew" even
before she reached the
kitchen.

"Katy, what's the matter?"
she asked, running into the
room. "What's that sound?"

Mother walked up to Katy and looked at the little gray kitten.

"I found it in the trash can, Mom," Katy quickly explained.

Mother recovered from her surprise, took the smelly kitten from her daughter, and began cleaning off the dried banana and other mysterious substances clinging to the kitten's fur.

"How do you suppose she got in the trash can?" asked Katy.

"Well, Honey," Mother began, "someone's cat probably had unwanted kittens. To get rid of this one, they must have thrown it in the trash."

"But that's mean!" said Katy. "They shouldn't have done that! Can we keep her, Mom? Can we?"

Mother was quiet for what seemed
like a long time to Katy.
First, she looked at her
daughter. Then she
looked at the
skinny pile
of gray fur.

Finally Mother spoke. "Katy, taking care of a cat is a big responsibility. You have to feed it and water it, housebreak it, and take it to the animal doctor for shots. If we do keep this stray kitten, you will have to be responsible for it."

"Then we can keep her, Mom?"

Katy scarcely heard another word. She was going to have her own pet, a beautiful gray kitten.

"I'll call her Allyson J. Cat, and I'll never tell anybody what the J. stands for."

"That's a funny name for a kitten," said Mother. "Allyson J. Cat ... ," she repeated. "On second thought, Ali is short for Allyson. And Ali Cat sounds like the perfect name for this one. Just don't forget that Ali Cat is your responsibility."

"I won't forget," promised Katy, giving Allyson J. a big hug.

The next day, Mother and Katy
bought a litter box, kitten food, and a
new little pink bowl. Katy couldn't
wait to show Allyson J.

Katy loved watching Allyson J. Cat eat a breakfast of kitten food from her new dish.

For the next three days, Katy checked Ali's water five times a day, gave her milk in a saucer, and kept her pink bowl filled with cat food.

On the fifth day, Katy was in a hurry and forgot to give Allyson J. her breakfast. But she remembered to fill the bowl by noon. And really, Allyson had plenty of water.

The next day, Katy forgot to give Ali Cat her food and water. She had been playing with her neighbor friend and having too much fun to think about her cat.

The next day she forgot too. Then the following day when Katy came down for breakfast, she found there was no place set for her at the table.

"Mommy," she yelled, "where's my bowl of cereal? And where's my juice?"

"Oh, that," said Mother. "I was so sleepy this morning, I guess I forgot about your breakfast. Go ahead and get what you want, Honey. I'm going back to bed."

Katy got her own bowl and spoon, but she couldn't reach her favorite cereal. She had to settle for Mom's good-for-you kind.

By the time Katy came in for lunch, she was hungry!

"Mom!" she yelled. "What's for lunch?"

"Oh, Katy, I'm sorry. I was so busy, I guess I forgot all about lunch. Better not count on me for dinner tonight either, Dear. I just don't know what I'll be doing."

Katy couldn't believe it.

"Mother, you have to feed me!" she said. "It's your job to feed me!"

Katy paused. "And it's your 'sponsibility too!"

Mother smiled and gave Katy a big hug.

"Yes, Katy, and, of course, I'll feed you. And Allyson J. Cat is your responsibility, isn't she?"

Katy realized that she hadn't kept her promise to take care of Allyson J.

"I'm sorry, Mommy."

"I think Ali Cat is the one who needs your apology," said Mom.

Katy ran over to her kitten, gave her
a hug, and filled her dishes.

"Allyson J., when God gave me a
kitty, He gave me a job. I'm sorry I let
you down. From now on, you're my
responsibility—and I'll take good care
of you!"

Ali rubbed against Katy and
answered with a deep "purrr-rrrr."

And
Katy knew
Allyson J. Cat
was saying
thank you.